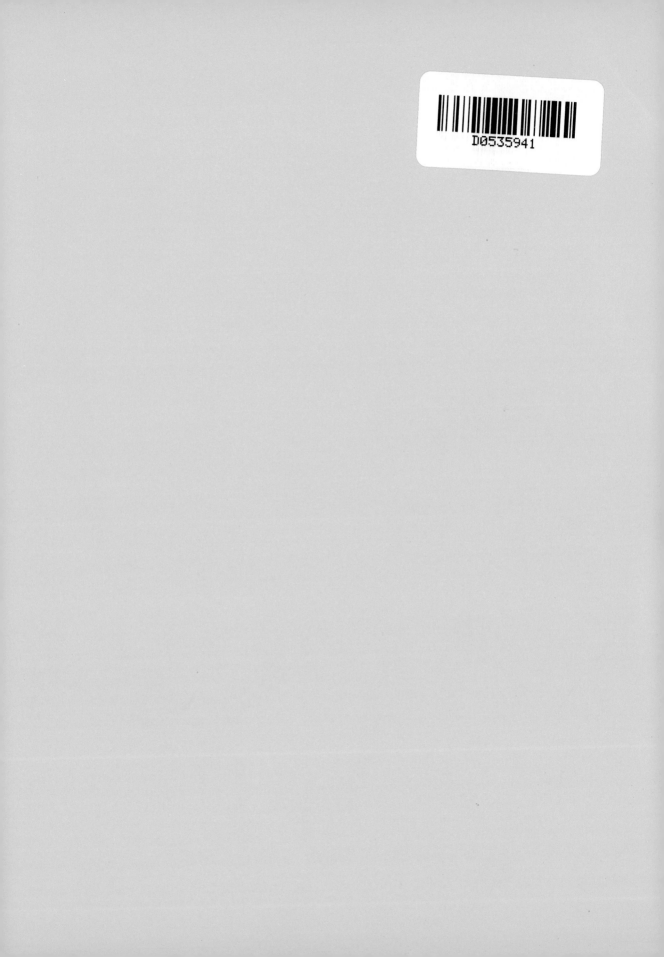

by Jess M. Brallier

pictures by Peter H. Reynolds

HARPER
An Imprint of HarperCollinsPublishers

To Tess M., who cared, imagined, and really did it;
she continues to inspire.
—J.M.B.

To my nephew Josh Reynolds, who at a young age
was inspired to save trees in his town and
around the world.
—P.H.R.

Tess's Tree
Text copyright © 2001, 2009 by Jess M. Brallier
Illustrations copyright © 2009 by Peter H. Reynolds

Manufactured in China.

Library of Congress Cataloging-in-Publication Data is available.
ISBN 978-0-06-168752-5 (trade bdg.) — ISBN 978-0-06-168753-2 (lib. bdg.)

Typography by Martha Rago
09 10 11 12 13 SCP 10 9 8 7 6 5 4 3 2 1 ❖ First Edition

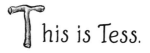
This is Tess.

This is Tess's tree.

Tess loved to swing from her tree, play in
its leaves, and camp out under it.
Tess loved her tree.

Tess was exactly 9 years, 3 months, and
2 days old.
Tess's tree was about 175 years old.
That's very old for a tree.

The leaves of Tess's tree grew green in the spring and turned yellow in the fall.

And long ago, the words "Tyler and Max" had been carved within the shape of a heart on the trunk of Tess's tree.

One night a storm blew hard
and long, making the tree's old
branches bend and shake.

A big branch fell
from Tess's tree.
And then another
one fell.

Tess's mom was worried. She said, "The tree could fall and hurt someone."
Not my tree! thought Tess.

But Tess's tree was taken down.

Tess was angry!
She threw her toys.

She screamed at the neighbors and
kicked the other trees.

Tess was sad. She hugged the branch
that used to hold her swing.

She lay on the stump of her tree and cried.
For a long time.

Tess had to do something for her tree.
She couldn't just let it quietly go away.

I know, she thought. My tree will
have a funeral.

Tess invited friends, family, and neighbors
to "Celebrate the Life of Tess's Tree."

Tess set up chairs and helped the children
of her tree dress up for the service.

When the service began, Tess walked
slowly to the stump of her tree.
    She laid a flower on it, wiped her nose,
and sat on the nearest chair.

A neighbor with a white collar said, "We, friends and family, are gathered here today to celebrate the life of Tess's tree."

Tess's teacher stood next to the stump and read a poem about a swing.

"How do you like to go up in a swing,
Up in the air so blue?
Oh, I do think it the pleasantest thing
Ever a child can do!"

Tess cried when she thought about
her tree and its swing.

A handsome husband and pretty wife
who looked like movie stars walked slowly
to the tree's stump.

"Dear friends of Tess's tree," said the wife, "I'm Tyler."

"And," said the husband, "I'm Max."

They looked at Tess and smiled.

"Wow!" Tess whispered. "It's them!"

"This was once our tree, too," Tyler said.
They each kissed Tess on her cheek.

An older woman walked unsteadily to the stump.

"My dear friends," the lady said. "This is me, as a child"—she held up an old photo—"more than seventy years ago, happily climbing among the branches of Tess's tree."

Awesome! thought Tess.

The old woman turned to Tess. "I loved your tree. Here, please, this is for you."

She handed the old photograph to Tess.

Tess's mother stood next to the stump and invited Tess to join her. She told the friends of Tess's tree how proud she was of her daughter. Tess smiled and thanked the people for helping to celebrate the life of her tree.

That night, Tess looked out her bedroom
window to where her tree once stood.

She thought about all her tree had done for so many people.

A last tear dried.
She was okay.